Maggie
THE BEAGLE and the **Oil Spill**

Have a tail/
wagging day.

Evelyn Hilmer

Maggie
THE BEAGLE
and the Oil Spill

Evelyn Gilmer

TATE PUBLISHING & *Enterprises*

Published by Tate Publishing & Enterprises, LLC
127 E. Trade Center Terrace | Mustang, Oklahoma 73064 USA
1.888.361.9473 | www.tatepublishing.com

Tate Publishing is committed to excellence in the publishing industry. The company reflects the philosophy established by the founders, based on Psalm 68:11,
"The Lord gave the word and great was the company of those who published it."

Book design copyright © 2011 by Tate Publishing, LLC. All rights reserved.
Cover & Interior design by Kellie Southerland
Illustrations by Benton Rudd

Published in the United States of America

ISBN: 978-1-61777-633-5
1. Juvenile Fiction: Animals: Dogs   2. Juvenile Fiction: Animals: Pets
11.05.17

*Dedicated to turtle volunteers who walk
the beaches daily and worked
tirelessly, transporting eggs away from the
oil-polluted waters of the Gulf Coast.*

Acknowledgement

Thanks to Mrs. Roberta Hudgins' fourth grade class.

Table of Contents

The Dead End Dogs

Maggie relaxed in her crate on the backseat of Ms. Evie's car. She sniffed the salt air and was excited about her upcoming fishing trip. Maggie was going to the beach to visit her canine cousins and go fishing. She loved her cousins and remembered the fun they always had together. Her cousins never mentioned her broken tail and Maggie loved them for that. No one knows how it broke except Maggie.

Ms. Evie's daughter, Julie, lived near the coast and had two dogs of her own, Baxter the Brute and Annabell Bella. The dog across the street from Miss Julie's was named Deer Leg Duke and all three dogs were affectionately referred to as the Dead End Dogs. That's because they lived at the end of the street and patrolled it daily. That gave them a sense of belonging and a feeling of importance. There were no pedigrees or blue blood lines to distinguish any of the crew. They were just a rag tag team of rescued animals who dreamed of someday becoming important. Important to the world, not just the family who loved them.

In preparation for the big event, "becoming important," the crew daily trained in Miss Julie's backyard. Strength training involved playing tug of war with an orange Frisbee. Covert spying and espionage entailed hiding the squeaky Martian and dressing up in disguises with towels from the swimming pool.

Baxter the Brute was an orange Basset hound with short legs. Miss Julie rescued him from a ditch where he had been abandoned. His left eye was permanently crossed at birth and his head tilted to the right when he looked at you. He was the strongest of the group and did his Superman stretch after each nap to stay in shape. Baxter didn't want anyone to make fun of his crossed eye and his greatest fear was that he would be left all alone by himself, again.

Baxter's little sister was Annabell Bella. She was a small white poodle who was born on Growler's Puppy Farm just like Maggie. Unfortunately, she suffered from seizures when she got excited. The vet prescribed pills that controlled the seizures and enabled her to live a normal life. Annabell wore a locket on her collar that kept the medicine with her at all times. She was the only female, fragile and needed to feel part of the crew.

Deer Leg Duke, the dog across the street, was a large yellow lab with a limp. He had been a prize winning hunting dog until he got hit by a car and broke his back left leg. Duke earned his name, Deer Leg because he drug around the leg of his owner's latest kill. The deer leg proved what a good hunter he still was and that made him feel important. He had poor personal hygiene and the deer

leg smelled awful! In spite of his limp and odor, Duke was jovial, lovable and happy to have friends.

Ms. Evie's son, Jon, was bringing his dog too. His name was Boo Man The Low Rider. Boo was a black dachshund with very short legs. Boo was the smartest cousin of all and so, he always had to be in charge. He wished his legs weren't so short, but he made up for it in brains. There would be lots of cousins to play with and Maggie was filled with excitement!

Maggie Goes Fishing

Ms. Evie's son, Jon, was a tournament-winning fisherman and scuba diver. He had invited Julie, Maggie and Ms. Evie to go fishing. There had been an oil spill in the Gulf of Mexico, and all the marine life was in danger. They wanted to fish before the oil spread near their beach.

Fishing was fun for Maggie, but the sun was hot. She stayed in the bow of the boat where there was lots of shade.

Ms. Evie put ice cubes in her water bowl to make sure Maggie was comfortable. She even had on her own "doggy life jacket" so she would be safe in case of an emergency.

Maggie listened as Jon talked about the oil spill and how polluted the Gulf was becoming. The oil company was not able to stop the flow of oil into the ocean. There had already been hundreds of fish, birds, and turtles washed ashore. Tar balls and gooey clumps of smelly oil had collected on the beautiful, white, sandy beaches. Jon was angry about the tragedy, and Miss Julie and Ms. Evie were sad. Jon wondered why someone could not solve the problem. So many fishermen depended on the waters for a living, and they were now out of work.

Maggie remembered the sea turtle nest she and Ms. Evie had watched hatch out three years ago. She thought about Squiggles, her favorite hatchling, and the eighty-four other baby turtles and wondered about their safety. How would they survive if they got oil in their lungs when they came up to breath? They couldn't see with gooey, polluted salt water in their eyes. Now Maggie was worried too!

Is That Squiggles?

Miss Julie had just cast her fishing line off the right side of the boat when something in the water caught her eye. What is that thing floating toward the boat? she thought. Jon saw it about the same time she did and shouted, "There's a turtle!" All eyes were on the oil-covered reptile as he struggled to swim toward the boat. He seemed to know the humans could help him and he was desperate. Jon grabbed his cell phone to call the Florida

Fish and Wildlife Commission, but the boat was too far off shore and there was no reception. Jon knew turtles were endangered and could only be handled by specially trained experts. Fortunately, Jon had taken all the classes and he was qualified to retrieve the struggling turtle. He grabbed his fishing net and leaned over the edge of the boat.

Maggie ran to the back of the boat and looked down into the salty ocean water. Even with all the oil covering the turtle's shell, Maggie spied the brown spot on his neck and recognized her friend Squiggles! Squiggles was the only turtle out of sixty-five hatchlings that had a brown spot on his neck. It had been three years ago when the turtle nest hatched out, but Maggie remembered it! She remembered

21

when he swam back as a baby to say thank you for helping them get safely to the water's edge. It was Squiggles! She barked and barked! How he found her in this big, huge gulf, Maggie would never know, but there he was! He needed her help again, and before Ms. Evie could stop Maggie, she jumped into the water and swam to greet him. It was then that everyone on the boat knew how special this turtle was to Maggie! Ms. Evie knew because of Maggie's reaction that the turtle had to be Squiggles.

The Size of a Dinner Plate

Jon was able to pull Maggie back into the boat. He gently lifted Squiggles to the clean towel Ms. Evie was holding. Miss Julie hurriedly got fresh water and a brush out of her beach bag. While Ms. Evie cradled Squiggles, Jon cleaned the nasty goo from the turtle's head and shell with mayonnaise from the lunch cooler. There was no Dawn detergent on the boat, and he knew the mayonnaise would

work. Maggie stayed close to Squiggles and whimpered attentively. Maggie knew Squiggles recognized her. He kept turning his head to look at his friend. He had grown over the past three years. He was the size of a dinner plate. But he never forgot Maggie, and she never forgot him. How in the world they managed to find each other was one of those rare miracles of Mother Nature.

Jon knew exactly what he had to do to save Squiggles. He turned the boat back to shore and headed straight for the rehab station. Scientists, researchers, and specially trained volunteers were providing portable collection shelters for all struggling, injured marine life. Swiftly getting Squiggles the help he needed saved his life. The volunteers cared for the turtle and provided the necessary emergency treatment. Maggie stayed close to Squiggles and no one dared object. Maggie gave a growl when needed, and it was understood that these two shared a special friendship and were not to be separated.

The scientist told Jon that Squiggles had come a long way to avoid the oil, but the polluted slick had spread faster than he could paddle. He told Jon that he had done the right thing and that Squiggles just needed a good cleaning and rest. The turtle would be taken across town to Marine World for rehabilitation. He would stay there until he could be transported to Cape Canaveral on the East Coast. Later he would be released along with all the other marine life.

Thousands of turtle eggs were being carefully dug up by scientists and placed in Styrofoam boxes. They were layered with the moist sand from their nests and shipped by special FedEx trucks to Cape Canaveral. There, NASA kept them in a climate-controlled room at eighty-five degrees until they hatched out. They would be released on the East Coast beaches, away from the polluted Gulf, and into the clean waters of the Atlantic Ocean.

The Puppy Posse

Ms. Evie and the scientist allowed Maggie to stay with Squiggles until he was stable and resting well. Miss Julie reminded Maggie that her cousins were waiting to play with her and they all went to her house for the evening. While Jon cooked one of his famous meals, Ms. Evie and Miss Julie talked about the chances of Squiggles and Maggie finding each other again after three years.

As soon as Maggie greeted her cousins she called everyone to the fort under Miss Julie's four-poster bed. It was a tight squeeze, and Duke was not happy to leave his deer leg outside. Maggie got down to business quickly. She told the story of Squiggles hatching out three years ago, how she and Ms. Evie had helped the baby turtles get safely to the water's edge, and how he was the only one who came back to say thank you! She explained the oil spill and finding him struggling in the ocean with goo all over him. Annabell cried and thought she just might have to take a pill from the medicine locket attached to her collar. Maggie continued to explain that Squiggles was at Marine World with plans to be taken to Cape Canaveral for release. Maggie could not let this happen! She could not lose her friend again, so the Dead End Dogs put their paws together and devised a covert plan of escape with the secret code name "S.S.," for Spring Squiggles!

Here was the chance all the dogs had dreamed of and trained for. This was the big event that would make them "Important!" Of course their group name should be changed. Yes, something powerful. Baxter thought of just the right name. "The Puppy Posse!" The cousins all agreed it was an awesome name!

Boo, the brains of the outfit, sent Duke in search of camouflage. Traveling across town to Marine World would require disguises. Under the cover of night, with the soft pitter patter of rain, the Puppy

Posse snuck out of the fort and through the back fence to Duke's backyard.

Annabell, the smallest, wore an old, camouflage, hunting hat that dragged the ground and completely covered her as she walked. Maggie draped a hunting jacket over her back and the sleeves flopped as she moved. A large, camouflage tarp hid Boo, Baxter, and Duke. If Boo and Baxter could stand the smell and talk Duke out of bringing the deer

leg, the Posse was ready to roll. The disguises were perfect, everyone thought. No one would ever see them!

Maggie led the way to Marine World. The Posse took a short cut through the woods. Baxter, the muscle, bit into the tarp, keeping it from sliding off the three dogs. No one spied the three humps plodding through the bushes, stopping now and then to take a potty break.

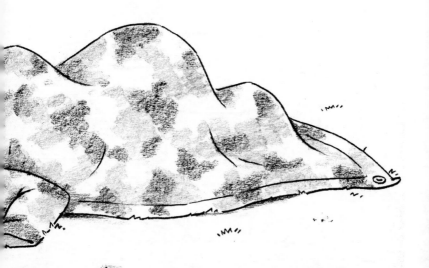

Crossing two streets was more of a challenge for the Posse. When the street light turned red, Maggie gave the signal. A camouflage hunting hat, jacket, and tarp bounced across the intersection, leaving motorists shaking their heads in disbelief. The disguises were genius! No one could explain to the police exactly what they had just seen.

Rent-a-Cop

Reaching Marine World was a relief for the canines. They stashed their disguises behind the ticket booth and sized up the situation. Marine World was basically three large buildings. Two buildings housed huge pools of salt water. The third building was an exhibit hall where all different kinds of marine life were displayed in their natural habitats. The buildings were connected with a covered walkway and the medical facility for the distressed marine life was in a room behind the first building.

Squiggles was in the first building, resting and regaining his strength in a small, plastic wading pool.

The game plan, they decided, was to move Squiggles to the third building where he could be in his natural habitat and live the rest of his life in safety. Never again would an oil spill endanger him. He would have plenty of food, and best of all, get to see Maggie and the Puppy Posse every Saturday when they came to visit. Squiggles would be used for educational purposes. School children would visit Marine World weekly and hear all about his life in the ocean. Stories of rescuing turtles from the oily, polluted Gulf waters would hopefully continue to serve as a reminder of how precious their marine life is and how fragile their environment remains.

After a short session of strategically laid plans, Duke slung his deer leg through a glass window and the Posse all jumped through. The breaking glass set off a silent alarm that summoned the Rent-a-Cop head of security. Annabell needed a pill for sure now; the excitement

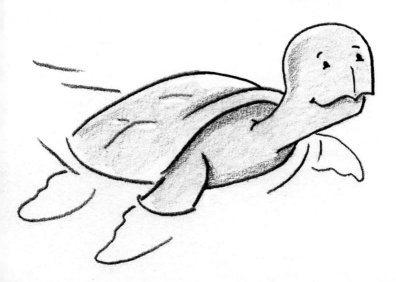

was too much for the tiny Bella. Inside the building, the canines quickly located Squiggles in a small wading pool. He was flapping his flippers, feeling much better, and thrilled to see the gang. Boo had given Baxter orders to get the tarp from behind the ticket booth. Maggie stepped on the side of the plastic pool, allowing Squiggles to paddle out and onto the tarp. Squiggles could be dragged along the walkway to the third building. But Squiggles couldn't go through a broken window! This covert plan would work perfectly if someone could just open the door! Just at that moment, a large figure appeared in the open doorway. It was Rent-a-Cop! The Posse's keen sense of fear caused every hair on every dog to stand at attention! What now?

In an instant, Maggie gave the signal! Boo, Annabell, and Maggie, bearing their teeth and barking, ran as fast as they could right at Rent-a-Cop. Baxter and Duke quickly dragged the tarp with Squiggles toward the open door. At this point, the Posse was acting on instinct. They didn't wait for code words or perfectly laid, covert plans. They did their thing! And as luck would have it, Rent-a-Cop fainted flat, dead away in the doorway! Squiggles and the Posse made it through the open door and down the walkway to the third building.

Getting through the last locked door was much easier this time. Boo had snatched the door keys from Rent-a-Cop's pocket as they slid past him, sprawled on the floor. They would have to work fast

before he woke up and foiled their plans. Duke managed to turn the key in the door and it easily swung open. Maggie led Squiggles to a nice pool where several other turtles were living. It took all five dogs to lift the turtle high enough to splash him into the salt water pool. The Puppy Posse watched as Squiggles swam over to a ledge and took a rest.

"Important" Volunteers

The Posse knew their work was finished. They had accomplished their goal. A high five went up among five very happy and tired dogs. Now, back in disguises, a hunting hat, hunting jacket, and camouflaged tarp bounced back to Miss Julie's house. They all five quietly snuck into the fort under Miss Julie's bed. Duke lost the vote, and the deer leg stayed outside in the back yard, but it had come in handy tonight, everyone had to agree. The Puppy Posse was looking forward to next Saturday and seeing their turtle friend, Squiggles, again. They fell asleep feeling good about being turtle volunteers in the oil spill. But, most of all, they finally felt important!

Squiggles was comfortable in his new, natural habitat where he would go unnoticed among the other turtles. He knew Maggie and her cousins had saved his life. As he remembered the oil spill and fearing for his life, tears filled his eyes. Maggie was truly his hero again and he couldn't wait to see her next week! Maggie was grateful for her canine cousins and all their help. She was grateful to Marine World for providing care for injured marine life. She was happy that school children would learn about turtles and how to protect endangered species for future generations. She was very grateful that Mother Nature led Squiggles to her boat so she could help him once again.

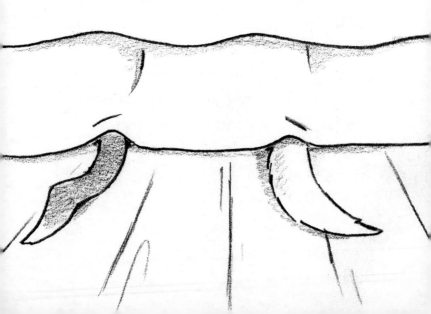

Maggie hadn't thought about her broken tail at all tonight. She was too busy being a turtle volunteer during the worst natural disaster in the history of the Gulf of Mexico. She was *Maggie Elizabeth,* a black-and-tan beagle with a broken tail.

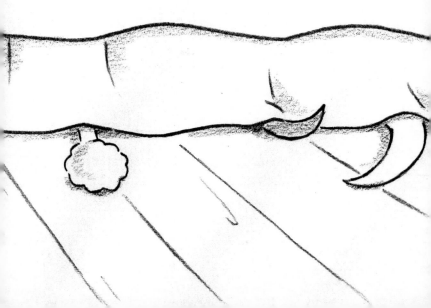